This book belongs to:

Amanda

Epstein

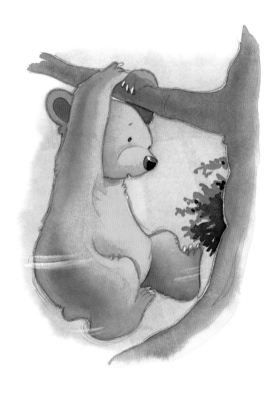

Written by Jillian Harker
Illustrated by Kristina Stephenson

© 2004 by Parragon Books Ltd

This 2007 edition published by Backpack Books,
by arrangement with Parragon Publishing.

ISBN-13: 978-0-7607-9213-1
ISBN-10: 0-7607-9213-5

Printed in China

10 9 8 7 6 5 4 3 2 1

I Love You, Mommy

p

"Watch me, Mommy," called Little Bear.
"I'm going fishing."

"Wait a minute," replied Mommy Bear.
"There's something you might want to know."

But Little Bear was already
running down to the river.

Mommy Bear ran too.

She saw Little
Bear jump onto
a rock.

She saw Little Bear
reach out his paw
to catch a fish.

Then Little Bear began to teeter and totter.

SPLASH!

"This doesn't feel so good!" thought Little Bear.

"Good try!" smiled Mommy Bear. "But you watch me now, Little Bear. I'll show you how to swim before you go fishing again." Little Bear watched Mommy Bear paddle all around.

"Your turn now, Little Bear," she said.

Little Bear did exactly what Mommy Bear had done.
"This feels good!" thought Little Bear.
"I love Mommy."

"Look at me, Mommy," called Little Bear.
"I'm going to pick those fruits."
"Just a minute," replied Mommy Bear.
"There's something you might want to know."

But Little Bear was
already climbing the tree.

Mommy Bear saw
Little Bear run
along a branch.

She saw Little Bear
reach out his paw to
pick a juicy fruit.

Then Little Bear began to *wibble* and *wobble*.

CRASH!

"This doesn't feel like fun!" thought Little Bear.

"Not bad!" said Mommy Bear. "But you look at me now, Little Bear. I'll show you how to climb properly before you go fruit-picking again."

Little Bear watched how Mommy Bear balanced as she climbed. "Your turn now, Little Bear," she said.

Little Bear did what Mommy Bear had done.
"This tastes good!" thought Little Bear.
"I love Mommy."

"Look, Mommy," smiled Little Bear. "All the other cubs are playing. I'm going to play, too." "Wait a minute, please," said Mommy Bear. "There's something you might want to know."

Little Bear stopped and turned.

"Tell me," he said.

"Be gentle when you play," said Mommy Bear.
"Look. Like this." Mommy Bear reached out her paws.
She wrapped her arms around Little Bear. She rolled
Little Bear over and over on the ground.

"I love Mommy," thought Little Bear. Then he ran off to play. He did just what Mommy Bear had done.

And it felt like fun!

Little Bear was very tired when he got home,
but there was something he wanted to say.
"I wanted to tell you," said Little Bear.
"What?" asked Mommy Bear.

"I love you, M..."
But Little Bear didn't finish.

Mommy Bear kissed Little Bear's sleepy head.

"I love you, too," she said.